Skye & Jacob

(Part 3)

A Hot & Steamy Aurelia Hilton's
Romance Short Novel Book 36

By Aurelia Hilton

Table of Contents

Chapter 1 Back to America *3*
Chapter 2 A Day in Seattle................................. *12*
Chapter 3 Storage Unit Surprises....................... *22*
Chapter 4: Homecoming................................... *29*
Let's Stay Connected . *Error! Bookmark not defined.*

Chapter 1 Back to America

I stood at the edge of the balcony attached to the room I shared with Jacob on his Yacht. It had become my regular spot whenever we neared land on the round the world trip we took after Jacob's computer worm crippled the Syndicate by stealing all of their accounts. It was a moonless night and as summer had given way to fall almost two months prior; I wore more than just a skimpy robe though the wind and drizzle bit through my warmer clothing

When Jacob initially suggested we continue around the world once we left Rome, I hadn't realized just how long the trip would be. Part of me assumed he wanted to keep me out of harm's way. The events in Rome shook him much more than they affected me. Since the Syndicate recruited me, I'd been used to danger. I even expected it to some extent, and I'd escaped harm, though I still had nightmares about the men I killed, even if they had been involved in one of Europe's biggest human smuggling rings.

The ship might have kept us physically apart from the world, but we had a satellite internet and tv connection. I'd kept in touch with the girls I'd saved in Rome. The Syndicate might have forced me to help them do great evil, but it was my own actions that brought their attention to me. I had a lot to make up for in this world and seeing those girls flourish now that they had been freed was a step in the right direction but I couldn't do more while I was still on this boat.

Not that I had many complaints about the trip outside its length. I'd traveled both Europe and Japan working for the syndicate in addition to going coast to coast in the United States but Jacob took me to so many places I'd never been before.

I fell in love with India in the few days we stayed there. I'd always loved the cuisine. As a teen in a small college town, the Indian restaurant was one of the few exotic places nearby though as I moved around to bigger and better cities as a con woman, I realized just how Americanized the Indian food from that restaurant really was. Even those metropolitan Indian restaurants paled in comparison to the food we had in India. I'd go back there in a second, just not on the damned boat.

The time together allowed for our relationship to flower as well. Before Jacob, I only regarded romantic feelings, at least in regard to men, as something to cultivate in them so that I could get what I wanted from them. They were a weakness I couldn't afford but it was different with Jacob. I cared for him, at least I thought I did. I'd held my heart closed for so long, I sometimes wondered if what I felt represented my real feelings or just my wishful thinking.

That was yet another reason I wanted off the boat. It is easy to find yourself feeling love towards a person when you are basically stuck with them almost 24/7 for months. Our relationship began on a bed of lies, on both sides, and while I thought our feelings were real, I knew that things would change once we were no long on our trip and the real world asserted itself again.

Lights appeared to either side of the yacht in the distance. Finally, we were back to the mainland of the United States. Well, the southern lights were in the United States. Victoria, the Capital City of British Columbia glimmered to the North. I shivered, and not from the cold. I worked a couple of cons in the Seattle area when I was independent and one for the Syndicate but I preferred to stay away. Seattle was too close to home.

I didn't leave my mother and stepfather's home in good circumstances and while I rarely returned; I kept in semi-regular contact with my mother. That changed when the Syndicate recruited me. As far as I knew, they didn't know my birth name, just the aliases I'd been using for years as I conned men from city to city. They would have killed me for going against them, the remnants of the group kidnapped me in Rome. I stopped contacting my mother after that, a little more than five years ago and until the Syndicate was truly dead and gone, I'd continue to stay away.

Were I as honest with myself as I would have liked, I'd admit I had more reasons than my mother's safety, in staying away. That I fell under the control of the Syndicate in the first place and what they forced me to do shamed me greatly. Waiting until I accomplished more against the remnants of the Syndicate before I returned home, something to offset the shame.

That said, the closer the ship got to Seattle the more I thought of home and regretted losing touch with my mother. As with my many other regrets, I tried to push them out of my mind though I knew, being this close to home, that was easier said than done. Thankfully, this visit should be short. We were going to Seattle to clear out the clothes in my storage unit, clothes purchased for me by a former mark, the scion of a prominent Seattle family-owned department store.

After that, I didn't know what we would do. Jacob had been cagey about the answer. I wanted to follow our initial plan, to take the fight to the remnants of the Syndicate and similar groups but I knew Jacob worried too much about my safety to stand by while I did what I needed to do. We'd need to have a long overdue conversation about that at some point.

Speak of the Devil, the door to our cabin opened behind me and Jacob joined me on the balcony. His arms slid around my waist as he pressed himself against me, shivering.

"How can you stand being out here," he said, his teeth rattling, "you feel so cold."

"I was born to it," I said, enjoying his warmth despite my words, "before my dad died and my mom remarried, I lived about an hour outside of Seattle. You get used to the drizzle, it happens 8 months of the year."

"Should I worry that you are sharing your past?" he asked, "you tend not to talk about it."

"I try not to think of it, but this close to home, that becomes more difficult," I replied, melting into his touch.

"If you ever want to go home," he said, his hands caressing my stomach, "I'd be more than happy to go with you. If that would help?"

"Thanks, but I want to wait until I know they'd be safe," I replied, "the Syndicate gave no indication of knowing my real name but I'd rather not risk her, just in case."

"I can understand that," he said, his hands exploring lower, "but I'm here if you want to talk about it or anything else."

"Don't want to find another Giovanni?" I teased with a wiggle of my hips. Jacob hadn't known his contact

7

in the Italian government was a former mark of mine, not before he recognized me. My arousal spiked thinking about how Jacob fucked me soon after that meeting.

Seeing a former lover of mine gave him the need to claim means he took me against the wall the moment the door to our hotel suite closed behind us. Raw and animalistic, I found it intoxicating. Not that our regular sex had been bad, he satisfied me better than all but the most skilled of my former marks, but sometimes I just want to be fucked. Times like this.

"You have any more Giovanni?" he asked, "any more surprises?"

"Surprises? I'm sure," I replied, "but I doubt we will meet a former mark, at least none as handsome as Giovanni."

Jacob growled and held me tighter, kissing my neck. Guilt tried to knock desire from its prominent position. Even with the feelings I had for the man, I still manipulated him to get what I wanted. Sure, from the way his cock poked against the small of my back, he wanted it too. No harm done, but given the sins of my past, I worried I'd be too willing to cross the line.

"I know one of your secrets," he whispered, kissing my neck, "you bring him up when you want a good fucking."

"Well," I said, wiggling my hips more to cover for my surprise, "are you going to give me what I want?"

If he knew what I was doing, it couldn't count as manipulation. My guilt faded away as the fog of our breath on this cold night, leaving only my desire for Jacob and to forget about nearing my home.

"You want it right here?" he asked, his breath hot on my neck, "it is warmer in the cabin."

"But it will be hotter here," I replied, pushing my ass out and arching my back.

He stumbled back a step, the hands on my lower stomach slipped to my hips. I shook my ass and he took the hint. One of his hands reached down and pulled my robe over my ass. His hands caressed my cheeks with only the leggings I wore as a barrier. Before long, his fingers grabbed the waistline and pulled them over my ass in a single strong tug.

"Gaaa," he said after he dropped his pajama pants, "the wind makes this a bit bracing."

"I know someplace warm," I said, pushing back with my hips.

He needed no further instructions and the head of his cock pressed against my slit, finding my waiting entrance. The hold on my hips strengthened as he thrust himself inside me, finding a rhythm that sped as he continued. I met his thrust, pushing against him.

"You are practically burning up," he said, his voice strained, "like an inferno."

"Maybe I was thinking about Giovanni," I said, "you know those Italian men."

With a grunt, his speed increased further and he slapped his hips against my ample ass with each one. I braced my arms against the railings as an orgasm hit me, pleasure radiating from where Jacob claimed me through the rest of my body. My knees when week as he continued and I neared a second orgasm in quick succession.

From his breathing, Jacob was close as well. Giving me one last, slow thrust, he held himself inside me. His cock jerked as he came, his cum almost too hot as it coated my insides.

Once it lost its hardness, his cock slipped out of me, and he dropped my robe down, pulling me back to a standing position. He hugged me from behind, as I continued to watch the distant shimmers of lights.

"Ok, it was kind of hot to do it out here," he said, "but it is way too cold, come back to the room. Come to bed. We will be in Seattle in the early morning and even you need your sleep."

In my post-orgasmic bliss, I let the worries fall away and joined him in our cabin. Being so close to home would bring worries and guilt back soon enough.

Chapter 2 A Day in Seattle

Something felt off when I woke up the next morning but I didn't discover what had changed until I slid out of Jacob's arms and out of the bed. There was no vibration to the floor and I realized the engines were off. I'd gotten so used to the constant hum in our last, long leg of the trip from Hawaii to Seattle that its absence seemed odd.

Back on my familiar balcony, I saw Seattle for the first time in two years. When my mother married my stepfather, we moved to Central Washington where he taught as a professor at Central Washington University. I hated it there: too cold in the winter, too hot in the summer and too far from Seattle.

Even before we moved, I dreamed of living in Seattle instead of the small suburban town an hour north. In sleepy Ellensburg, those dreams only intensified. Seeing it now, after all these years and all the cities I'd lived in, Seattle still brings nostalgic feelings even if I'd only lived in the city for less than half a year.

I compared every city I go to against my childhood favorite and found them lacking. Sure, other cities beat Seattle. New York had better food, Paris better art, Tokyo better public transportation, Los Angeles a better climate, but I loved Seattle more.

"I don't think I've ever seen you smile like that," said Jacob from my side.

I flinched at his words. One of the skills I'd hired in my years with the Syndicate was a sense of my surroundings. Things worked better when there were no surprises. So, caught up in looking at Seattle, I missed his entrance.

"We could move here if you like," he said, sliding his hand over my shoulder, "with what we took from the Syndicate, it isn't like we ever need to work again."

My smile only grew at the thought of moving back to Seattle, sharing my favorite city with Jacob. I wanted nothing more, but reality reasserted itself.

"Once we are certain the remnants of the Syndicate are gone, I'd like that," I said, "I could show you all my favorite places."

"Why don't we hit up a few places today," he said, "I've only been to Seattle for business, I've never even been in the Space Needle."

"That's a bit touristy for locals," I replied, "but I haven't been there since I was a kid. It might be fun to pretend to be a tourist for a day."

It was fun. We went to the top of the Space Needle then had lunch at Public Market. One of the benefits of playing the tourist was that these tended to be

13

away from the parts of the city I spent most of my time in. They didn't bring back memories or the worry and guilt that came with them.

For dinner, I chose a dive bar I used to go to with my con woman mentor Claire as a teen. I had my first drink there, thanks to a fake ID Claire had made for me, an 18th birthday present. She was a student at Central Washington University while I was in high school when we met and she had a car. We came to Seattle often, except in winter. Her car couldn't handle the mountain pass.

Coming back to the dive bar brought all the memories of that first time here. Memories of Claire and that night flooded me, memories of the kiss we shared afterward and how our friendship turned to more. Before I met Jacob and fell for him, Claire might have been the only person I ever loved in that way.

"You look lost in thought," said Jacob, almost yelling to cut through the sound of the music, "memories of this place."

"Yeah," I replied, "I had my first drink here, lots of memories."

"Hope they are good ones," he said, taking a sip of his beer.

"Mostly," I replied, truthfully. The bad memories from my relationship with Claire came later when we parted ways professionally and personally over my desire for bigger scores. That break up led me to take bigger risks and falling under the control of the Syndicate but it also brought me to Jacob in the end. I regretted the hell out of a lot of it, but I liked where it took me.

Even so, before I met Jacob, before I helped him destroy the Syndicate, I often fantasized about how my life would have turned out had I stayed with Claire. I could have been happy with her, I know that. I was happy with her, for a time. But I was happy with Jacob now and with what we planned to do to the remnants of the Syndicate.

"But given what I've done in my life, even my happiest memories have a bit of a cloud to them," I said, picking up my own beer glass.

"We need to make new memories to cover the old," he said, "if we moved here, we could do that every day."

"There is a lot of work to do before then," I said.

"Is there?" he asked, drawing my suspicion, "after Rome, Giovanni brought Interpol into his operation. You've read the same reports I have, the remnants in Europe are all but destroyed."

"They had their fingers into 6 continents," I replied, "with Europe gone that leaves five more."

"And Interpol will work with local authorities in those continents and continue the fight," he said, "it doesn't have to be you."

"I want it to be me," I barked, "I need it to be me. They forced me to help them, help them hurt people. Taking them down is the first step in making that right, doing the right thing."

"There are so many other good things you can do," he argued, placing his hand over mine, "and you've done so much already. We destroyed the syndicate, forced its operatives to scrabble for the remains and what about the girls in Rome? Without you... I don't want to think what would have happened to them if you were not there."

"It isn't enough," I said, shaking my head, "if I can help take down the remnants, I will."

"I want you to help, I really do," he said, squeezing my hand, "but these are dangerous people. They kidnapped you..."

"Attempted to abduct me," I said, continuing a disagreement that has been going on since the events happened, "I am an adult and I got away from them with all those girls, that is an attempted abduction."

"Thugs pulled guns on you and forced you into the catacombs under Rome," he replied with his standard line, "once they take you to a second location, you have been kidnapped."

"Abducted," I interrupted, noticing the ghost of a smile on his face, "you were arguing with ulterior motives?"

"Guilty as charged," he replied, his smile growing, "I knew if I brought up your kidnap…"

"Abduction."

"Abduction," he continued, "it would distract you from your memories. You are not the only one who knows how to manipulate people."

"Where did you learn that?" I asked.

"I learned it from watching you, dad," he said, to which I furrowed my brows. He shook his head and continued, "it's a reference to an anti-drug commercial from the 80s. Thank you for making me feel old by not getting it."

"Thank you for trying to keep me from drowning in my memories," I said, adding my other hand to where he held mine, "old timer."

After dinner, we went to a jazz club. When I first heard jazz, I didn't understand its appeal. Several of the men I conned had an interest and I'd assumed it was one of those things rich people like because it was sophisticated. They liked it because Frasier Crane talked about it on reruns. One expected me to like it and be conversant in it so I began to listen to some classics. A few albums later, I kind of dug it, at least the classics. Some of the more out there artists sounded more like noise to my uncultured ears.

The club featured a vocalist singing his own words to jazz standards. It banished the more maudlin memories that my choice of dinner spot brought. Well, that and the bottle of wine we shared while listening.

By the time the car reached our hotel for the night, I was feeling frisky. Part of me wondered if it came from the memories of my relationship with Claire coming to the foreground. Thankfully, the wine I drank kept those thoughts from dominating but I basically attacked Jacob when the elevator door closed.

We kissed, his hands roaming my body, slipping under my coat. The elevator dinged and opened well before the penthouse and we pushed apart, trying to pretend we weren't less than 30 seconds from fucking in the elevator. My straight face beat Jacob's but I knew it was flushed and my breathing just a tad heavy.

An older couple entered the elevator, the woman studying our faces with an inquisitive eye. They left the elevator a few floors later and we burst into laughter when the doors closed after them only to begin a heated kiss a moment later.

My hands slid down to his crotch, caressing his hardness through his suit pants. I dropped to my knees, intent on blowing him, at least making him think I would blow him in the elevator.

"Wait for the room," he said, his eyes wide as he tugged on my shoulder for me to stand, "what if someone gets on the elevator?"

"I just wanted to give the security guards a nice show," I said, standing and waving to the camera on the ceiling.

"Security guards?" he squeaked, looking at the camera but his expression shifted to a slight smile, "you don't think they are watching."

His cock jerked in his pants, confirming what I thought and I captured his lips in a kiss. As with last night when we fucked on the balcony of his yacht, I'd noticed several times since we'd been together that he got excited by exhibitionism but just a little bit.

We broke the kiss to leave the elevator and the second we entered the suite before he had even closed the door, I dropped to my knees, undoing his belt. I ripped his pants and boxers down, freeing his hard cock. Grabbing it with both hands, I leaned in and gave the head a lick before taking it into my mouth.

I'd never liked the way men smell but when Jacob's musky sweaty scent hit my nose, I liked it, it excited me. Were I completely sober, I'd question just when this change happened but tipsy as I was, I just enjoyed it as I bobbed up and down on his cock, licking as much as I could, my hands working the base of his shaft.

"I don't know what I did to deserve this," said Jacob between panting breaths, "but I'm not going to complain. You have a talented tongue."

I looked him the eye and winked in response. He'd helped me so much between his plan to destroy the Syndicate and when the thoughts of my past threaten to overwhelm me. I still questioned if I were capable of love, but I knew that if I was, I loved Jacob and wanted to show it.

"I'm going to cum," he warned.

I continued with my tongue and mouth but squeezed the base of his cock to elongate the orgasm. Finally, his breath ragged, he braced himself on my shoulders and his cock spasmed in my mouth, his salty cum splashing across my tongue.

When I kept going, he pulled his softening cock from my mouth and helped me to my feet.

"You know, and I'm not saying this because of the amazing blow job," he said, not making eye contact, "but I love you, Skye."

He turned to look at me after he said my name, vulnerability and need all over his face.

"I love you too," I said for the countless time to a man.

For the first time in my life, I think I actually meant it.

Chapter 3 Storage Unit Surprises

Dreams of my past plagued my sleep that night, dreams of Claire. I lived through the evening of our first kiss, tasting the cheap beer and greasy bar food on her lips. My dreams moved forward in time to when I pushed her to go further with the cons, when I pushed too far for her to follow, finally pushing her away.

Leaving her, pursuing some of my bigger scores was probably the greatest regret of my life and until I met Jacob and helped him destroy the Syndicate, I wanted nothing more than to take it back. As if sensing this, my dreams showed me an alternate version of my life, one where I stayed with Claire, found love in her arms and never found myself on the Syndicate's radar.

I saw us pulling the little scams and cons that Claire taught me. In the dream, we didn't have much money, certainly not as much as I had now with the partnership with Jacob but we were happy and my conscience untroubled by the greater sins of the Syndicate.

The dream of the alternate universe faded as I woke with a start, realizing how hollow it truly was. Sure, had I never left Claire, I could have been happy but looking back with the experiences I'd gained from my time under the Syndicate's thumb, that life with Claire no longer appeals to me and not just because of the money I now had.

I'm self-aware enough to understand that greed is one of my primary motivators. I used my abilities to manipulate men for the purpose of easy money and when I discovered I could get more by extorting them, my greed pushed me along. My greed led me to leave Claire when she wouldn't go along with my extortion plans. My greed helped the Syndicate discover and use me. Hell, half the reason I agreed with Jacob's crazy plan to drain the Syndicate's accounts was his promise to share the proceeds with me.

After he agreed to split them 50/50, I no longer had a need for my greedy impulses. They still existed, the small voice in the back of my mind that continued to look out for number 1. Instead of greed, the desire to make restitution, to make up for the sins of my past shifted into prominence. The life with Claire my dreams showed me lacked that desire. It took hitting rock bottom, falling prey to the Syndicate, for the conscience in my shriveled black heart to reassert itself.

Leaving Claire, I caused a lot more evil to happen in the world, but now, with the resources and knowledge at my command, I had a chance not only to make up for the evil I did but to do even more good. Plus, I had Jacob.

Before Jacob, I'd never considered men more than marks. They existed solely for the resources I could take from them. I'd had minor crushes on a few of my marks in the past, but I'd locked my inner romantic in a cage after I parted with Claire and never expected anyone, let alone a man, to pry it open.

Fully awake now, I slipped out of the humongous bed quietly to not disturb Jacob. The shades were open and after wrapping a robe around my naked body; I stepped out onto the balcony, ignoring the freezing concrete under my bare feet. A panoramic view of Puget Sound in the predawn gloom of a Seattle November opened up before me and I stared over the dark water, watching a ferry boat approach its dock below me.

I watched the activity on the dark water until the sky to the east began to lighten as the rays of the rising sun spilled around the distant mountains. Clouds soon marred the sunrise, obscuring the sun and darkening the sky. Drizzle fell and I turned to return to the suite.

Jacob stirred but didn't wake when I walked past, heading for the bathroom. By the time I stepped out, freshly showered, he was awake and greeted me with a hug and kiss to the cheek before he stepped into the bathroom for his own shower.

Today we planned to clear out my storage unit. Jacob hired a moving company and truck to handle the actual work, but I still dressed in jeans and a tourist T-shirt I picked up in the Azores covered with a light jacket. I'd like to be able to help if need be.

Once Jacob finished and dressed, in a suit like he always wore, we headed downstairs for a quick breakfast before departing to meet the movers at the storage unit, south of Seattle. Jacob rented a Tesla Roadster for the day.

"I've been thinking about buying one," he said when I asked him about it, "so I figured I should try it out."

"I didn't know y0u could rent such an expensive car," I replied, though I had little experience renting cars.

"Oh, there are companies that rent almost anything," he replied, "for a price. Everything has a price."

The moving truck beat us to the storage unit but only I had the key, so they mulled outside. The door rolled open, and I immediately noticed something that shouldn't be there, an envelope someone slipped under the door. Scrawled on the letter in red marker was 'Foul Temptress' with a smiley face next to it.

I didn't need to recognize the handwriting to know the letter was from Claire. Only she called me that, once she discovered my natural talent at manipulating men. I tore open the envelope to read the message.

"Sarah," the letter started in Claire's neat handwriting, "I didn't know how to contact you but I found this storage unit rented in your name so I hope this note gets to you. Your mother has been diagnosed with cancer and doesn't have long to live. Please visit her if you get this letter."

A tear ran down my cheek as I continued to read, "Sarah, I've missed you more than anything and I would love to see you again. We both said a lot of things when we parted and speaking for myself, I regret what I said…"

I crumpled the letter as more tears fell, thinking more about my mother than about Claire. I wanted to wait until I knew she would be safe before visiting my mother but if she didn't have much time left, I'd have to go soon.

"What was it?" Jacob asked, putting his hand on my shoulder.

"The letter was from Claire," I said, "my mother has cancer, not much time."

"How long has the letter been here?" he asked, "It's been a couple of years since you have been here.

I uncrumpled the letter to look for a date. Claire put the date next to her signature at the bottom: September 12th of this year.

"Two months ago," I replied, "I need to go see her. If we leave now, we can be there this afternoon."

"Of course," he said, squeezing my shoulder, "the movers can pack all of this stuff."

"Go start the car," I said, "I need to grab something here first."

His expression switched to suspicious for a fraction of a second before he smiled and nodded, moving to talk to the head mover then back to the car. I slipped past the hanging racks of clothes, pulling a long winter coat off its hanger as I passed. There would be snow on the ground in Ellensburg.

Past the racks of clothes, I kneeled in front of a duffle bag. I found what I needed the moment I unzipped the bag: a small pistol. It wasn't that I didn't trust Claire's letter, but I wanted to be prepared should something go wrong. After checking that it was loaded, I double checked the safety and stashed it in my purse.

Jacob had the Tesla pulled up to the door by the time I exited the storage unit and let the movers start to pack the substantial wardrobe I had there. His focus on the navigation screen of the vehicle he jolted when I opened the door.

"I've got the sat nav set for Ellensburg," he said, "it says we can be there in two hours."

"We have to get a different car first," I said.

"What?" he asked, not wanting to turn in the car he'd quickly fallen in love with, "it has more than enough range."

"I'm not worried about the range," I replied, "we have a mountain pass to cross and this car would stand out too much. I'd rather keep a low profile."

"Those are good reasons," he said, moping, "at least I get to drive it back to the rental agency."

I jolted against the back of the seat as he took off.

Chapter 4: Homecoming

Two hours later we crested the pass through the cascade mountains that split the state in half with me driving the rented SUV. Jacob tried to convince me to rent one of the SUVs from the company he rented the Tesla from but a $200,000 SUV would stand out as much as the $200,000 roadster. Not so with the common domestic model she chose.

I'd driven over the pass in much worse weather, but the snowy conditions required enough thought to banish my growing guilt over cutting myself off from my mother and the fear that I received Claire's letter too late to see my mother again.

Even with the fears over her safety due to the Syndicate, I could have reached out. Once Jacob and I put his plan into motion, I should have reached out to her. I'm a resourceful woman, I knew several ways that I could have contacted her, let her contact me without anyone else knowing about it.

Before thinking about it, I realized the real reason I didn't contact her: shame over my actions. I'd done so many dark things and I couldn't bear the thought of her judging me by those actions, I'd wanted to make up for them, to do good before I came home. Now, knowing she was sick, those reasons seem childish and selfish.

"You should probably slow down," said Jacob from the passenger seat, his fingers white where they gripped the handgrip over the door. It was the third time he'd said it in the last hour.

"Sorry," I said, lifting my foot from the pedal.

"Remember that getting pulled over will take a lot more time than driving the speed limit," he said, again for the third time.

"You didn't seem to care about the speed limit in that Tesla," I said.

"There wasn't any snow on the ground," he replied.

"This is nothing," I said, "Claire had a rear wheel drive car, and we crossed the pass when it was only open for cars with studded tires."

"That doesn't fill me with confidence," he said, watching me as I continued driving, "I'm here if you want to talk about anything. I'm here for you."

I smiled and placed a hand on his knee, giving it a squeeze.

"Both hands on the wheel," he said and I rolled my eyes.

"With our money, we should be able to get her the best care," he said, "assuming that the cancer is treatable, we will make sure she survives."

"I'd been thinking along the same line," I said, "it is the least I could do after disappearing from her life for five years."

"You had good reasons," he said, "if the Syndicate knew about her, they could have used that knowledge against you, hurt her to get to you."

"That doesn't make me feel better about it though," I replied.

"How did Claire find your storage unit?" he asked, pausing before he said her name. I'd brought her up but hadn't exactly told him about the extent of our past relationship.

"I used my real name to rent it," I said, trying to keep my voice disinterested, "the Syndicate did not know my real name, at least I think, so it was a bit of an escape hatch. I had the clothes my old mark gifted me and a go bag."

"A go bag?" he asked, "what's that."

"A bag ready for travel at a moment's notice," I replied, "should the shit go down, I'd find my way to the storage unit, grab the go bag and... well, go."

"Where to?" he asked, "if you had to go now, where would you go?"

"It isn't just me anymore," I replied, "it's something we would both have to agree on now. But when I made my first go bag, somewhere in southeast Asia. Somewhere cheap with good food and as far from the Syndicate as I could get."

"Should I pack a go bag?" he asked, and I shook my head.

"You have a yacht," I replied, "that is a multimillion dollar go bag right there."

Once off the pass and nearing the city I spent my teens in, things become more and more familiar and the guilt gnawing at my insides grew exponentially. I fidgeted in my seat when we took the exit off the freeway and my breathing quickened as I turned on the familiar road.

"That's the house," I said, pointing to the snow-covered two-story house as we drove by.

"Why are we not stopping?" he asked, straining his neck to look back at the house, "there was parking all along the street."

"I didn't survive five years under the Syndicate by being sloppy," I said, "there is a chance they got the Claire and the note is a ruse. Best we park a couple of blocks away and walk, just in case her house is being watched."

"I always love when you start acting like a spy," he said, taking my hand as we walked back the way we came, "my own sexy lady James Bond."

"You don't make a good Bond Girl," I said, "but that's probably a good thing, they tend to die."

We fell silent for the rest of the short walk. Memories and nostalgia hit me with almost every step. As much as I always wanted to leave this small town, I made a lot of memories here, many of them good. I stopped in the sidewalk in front of my Mother's house, staring at it as guilt ate away at my insides.

It looked almost exactly the same as when I left, down to the snow-covered roof and yard. I'd had an argument with my Stepfather packed my bag and left, screaming and yelling at both him and my mother. I'd turned 18 in October though I still had to finish my senior year in Highschool. Claire was a sophomore at the university and I moved into her apartment. I came back a few times, repaired my relationship with both my mother and stepfather, but I never lived in the house again after that.

"If you are worried the house is being watched, standing out front like this will bring their suspicion," Jacob said, pulling me towards the door, "it's best to rip the bandage off in situations like this."

I let him drag me to the porch where I knocked on the door. It took all my willpower and Jacob's firm grip of my hand to not bolt from the porch. My mother opened the door and regarded us for a second before her eyes focused on me, narrowing slightly as she tilted her head. It might have been five years since I talked to her, but I hadn't seen her in six and her aging seemed exaggerated, crow's feet around her eyes and a few more wrinkles than I remembered marred her face. Her hair was still the vibrant curly brown that I shared with her though I'd continued to keep mine dyed platinum blonde since the Azores.

"Sa... Sarah?" she asked, her curious expression morphing into one of surprise, "is it really you?"

I nodded, as unshed tears filled my eyes and she pulled me into a strong hug, the scent of her perfume filling my nose, smelling like home.

"Come in, come in," she said, pulling back from the hug, unshed tears glistening in her own eyes.
She turned to Jacob and they narrowed again, "and who is your friend?"

"This is Jacob, Mom," I replied, "we're together."

"I thought you liked girls?" she asked, "you were with that Claire girl."

"That was a long time ago, Mom," I replied, noticing Jacob's widened eyes. I really needed to learn how to share things with him before they get sprung on him.

"We thought you were dead," my mother said, anger lacing her voice, "it's been over five years without a single visit or even a call and then the FBI showed up, we thought you were dead."

"The FBI?" I asked, "when did that happen?"

"This summer," she replied, "your stepfather and I were enjoying a nice lunch when they started banging on the door. They asked all sorts of questions. Where were you? Who were you working for?"

"Did they tell you why they were looking for me?" I asked, wondering if I was wrong about the Syndicate not knowing what my real name was.

"They said they found your DNA at a crime scene in New York City," she replied, "some missing millionaire, Simmons I think,"

"Simons," I interrupted, my eyes turned from my mother to Jacob who looked away. I hadn't known the FBI had been looking for me but I could imagine the type of DNA they found in Jacob's bed.

"They said they would come back with more questions but they never did," my mother continued, looking between me and Jacob, "I heard on the news that they found him. He left New York City before the gunmen stormed his apartment."

"To be fair, I didn't know the FBI was looking for you when I told them I wasn't missing," said Jacob.

"You?" asked my mother, her eyes studying Jacob, "it was your apartment?"

"Yes," he said, holding out his hand, "Jacob Simons. It is a pleasure to meet you, even in such unfortunate circumstances."

"What are you talking about," she asked.

"If the FBI knew who I really was, the remnants of the Syndicate could easily find out," I said, moving to the window, peeking outside, "Claire's letter must have been a fake. You don't have cancer, do you, mom?"

"Cancer? What are you talking about? What letter?" she asked, "Claire came by a few months ago but we didn't know where you were. We couldn't help her find you."

"Shit, shit, shit, it was a trap" I muttered as I watched a car pulled up across the street, "Mom, call 911, go upstairs and get into the bathtub."

I stepped back from the window and pulled the gun out of my purse, flipping the safety off. Both my mother and Jacob stared at the pistol in my hand.

"Why do you have a gun?" my mother asked.

"Mom," I repeated, "911, upstairs, bathtub. Now! I'll explain everything when you are safe."

She opened her mouth as if she was going to say something else but the expression on my face stopped her. She picked her phone up from the table and rushed upstairs. Jacob discreetly looked out the window, his eyes going wide before he retreated.

"I'd ask where you got the gun," he said, "but I'm glad that you have it. What's the plan?"

"You, my mother or myself not dying is the extent of it at the moment," I replied, "keep away from the windows, I don't know how hot these guys are going to be coming."

Jacob stepped further into the house, standing behind the china cabinet in the dining room, peeking out to the front of the house. I ducked behind the cabinet on the other side, my gun at the ready.

Heavy footsteps sounded on the porch and someone banged repeatedly on the door.

"We know you are in there," a deep voice yelled through the door, "nobody has to die today. If our employer gets their money back, you can walk away, both of you."

Jacob and I looked at each other, both of us rolling our eyes. They would be more than happy to take the money back, but even if we complied, they would still kill us. It was a deterrence to others who would consider the same act.

Criminals can't go to the cops when someone steals from them, they can't go to court to enforce a breached contract. All they can do is enforce it themselves, from the barrel of a gun if need be. We'd stolen a hell of a lot from the Syndicate, so much that it mortally crippled the organization. They wouldn't let that slide.

"The cops are on their way," I yelled, "do you know how trigger-happy rural cops are? You should leave while you still have the chance."

The door shook with a sudden bang, they were trying to kick it down. A second bang sounded, and the door shook further, cracking around the deadbolt. I held my gun up, waiting for the door to break.

The next kick blew the door open. It slammed against the wall, bouncing back before she could take a shot at the man on the porch. He pushed the door open

with one hand, holding a pistol on the other. I didn't
give him a chance to use it.

I squeezed the trigger twice, my ears ringing from the
sound. The man fell after the second shot and I
ducked back behind the cabinet, expecting his partner
to retaliate. I didn't have to wait long, the roar of his
gun sounding as he shot blindly into the house.

Sirens in the distance were the only sounds for a
moment after he emptied his clip. I glanced over to
Jacob who huddled behind the other cabinet,
physically unharmed. A car door slammed and then
an engine started, tires squealing. I guessed that the
other man fled, but I remained cautious.

I stepped out from behind the cabinet, my gun at the
ready just in case. The car across the street was gone
and nobody else popped out to shoot me. I stashed
my gun back in my purse walked up to the man I
shot.

"Jacob, it's over. We need to get out of here," I said,
patting the dead man's pockets, "we don't want to be
here when the cops come."

"You, you killed a man," said Jacob, "in self-defense,
but if we leave now the cops will be after you."

"If the Syndicate can find me here, they can find me
at the police station," I replied, fishing a motel

keycard out of the dead man's pocket, "we are going to take the fight to them first."

"Is he dead?" asked my mom from the stairs, her phone in her hand.

"Sorry for the mess, mom," I said, taking Jacob's hand and pulling him out the door as the sirens got louder, "I shouldn't have come back. It wasn't safe."

I turned and hurried out the door, dragging the still shocked Jacob behind me. I killed my first person in Rome but in my previous line of work, I'd had guns pointed at me on more than one occasion. Jacob fought his war against the Syndicate from behind a computer screen. I could understand his reaction to being shot at, but at the moment I didn't have time for it.

Halfway down the block, he snapped out of his shock and I didn't have to continue to drag him. A pro tip for leaving the scene of a crime is not to run. Guilty people run and since the cops were coming, I didn't want us looking guilty. We walked, quickly, but still walking. Another pro tip, one that Jacob hadn't learned, is to ignore any cop cars unless that actually try to stop you.

We had just reached our rental SUV when a cop car barreled down the road. I continued to the car as I normally would but Jacob dropped down behind the wheel well of the SUV. I prayed that the cop didn't notice, but as usual, my prayers were not answered.

The cop car came to a screeching halt, circling in the nearby intersection. If we got out of this, I would have to teach Jacob how to handle himself when the shit went down. We were almost home free before he did that.

The Cop pulled up in front of our rental and he stepped out. The man looked vaguely familiar but with the cowboy hat and mirrored sunglasses, I couldn't quite place him. He stepped around the door to his cruiser, one hand looped on his belt near his gun. His eyes found Jacob who fidgeted under such scrutiny, another pro tip to give him later if we didn't get arrested right now.

"Officer, we heard gunshots that way," I said, with an intentionally frantic tone, pointing back towards my mother's house.

"We have cars at the scene already," he said, his eyebrows lowering below his sunglasses as he looked at me, before turning to Jacob, "why were you hiding from me? Did you have anything to do with this?"

"He's terrified," I said, answering for the stymied Jacob, "we've never heard a shooting."

"Can you answer for yourself, Sir?" the cop asked after giving me another odd look. Given the familiarity I felt towards the man, he had to recognize me as well, at least a little. I only knew one cop from my time in Ellensburg, and he was far too old to be the cop standing in front of them.

"The gunshots scared me," said Jacob. I wouldn't have to teach him everything about being in a crisis.

"That doesn't explain why you were trying to hide from the police," the cop said, turning his attention to me, "I swear I recognize you but I just can't place you."

"You don't recognize me, I have one of those faces," I said, turning to Jacob, "Isn't that right, honey? People always think the recognize me?"

"Yeah," he said, smiling at me, "you do have one of those faces."

"See," I said, shrugging, "sorry for the confusion."

The cop stared and took a step towards us to get a better look. He shook his head and took another step and I could read the nameplate on his uniform: Michael Stewart. I went to high school and his dad was the cop. He recognized me as well, his eyebrows shot high above his sunglasses and he snapped his fingers, pointing at me.

"Sarah?" he asked, taking a step back, his hand on his gun, "it is you, Sarah. The call came from your mother. What the hell is going on? Did you know the FBI was sniffing around during this summer looking for you?"

"There are people after me, after us, Mike," I said, holding my hands up to my sides, "they came for me when I visited my mother."

"Shit, Sarah, I need to bring you in for questioning then," he said, reaching for his radio.

"If you take us in the people who are after me would target the station," I said, shaking my head, "I already put my mother at risk, I don't want anyone else to be targeted because of me."

"The police have to be able to protect you," he countered, "it's our damn job."

"I'm not discounting that," I replied, "but these are dangerous people and I think they took Claire."

"My dad always said that girl was trouble," he said, "but I haven't seen her around since she graduated. What do you plan to do about it? I can't have people taking the law into their own hands."

"I just want to find her, make sure that she is OK," I replied, "once I know she is safe, I'll disappear until it is safe. You won't have to worry about me or any of my problems."

"Can you at least tell me what this is about?" he asked.

"We crippled their criminal organization," said Jacob, joining the conversation for the first time, "and those that still have power want to stop us from doing it to them as well."

"And you are?" Mike asked of Jacob, his eyes studying the man.

"Jacob Simons," he said, extending his hand to shake before realizing the situation and dropping it.

"You're the guy from New York City the feds were all worried about," Mike said, turning back to me, "they thought you had something to do with his disappearance. Found your DNA in his penthouse."

"My mother told me," I said, "and the men who stormed his apartment work for the same people who are after us."

"I don't like this at all," he said, shaking his head but moving his hand away from his gun, "but I believe you. Get going, but you are going to meet me after dark at the lookout and answer more of my questions. I'll see what I can find at your mom's house."

"Thank you, Mike," I replied, moving towards our rental, motioning Jacob with my head to follow, "we'll be there."

I took off before Jacob even fastened his seatbelt, heading for the freeway entrance. I'd keep my word to Mike, but we had hours before dark and I wanted to make sure we weren't tailed.

"Your crisis acting needs a little work," I said after silence reigned for a long moment, "if I hadn't gone to school with Mike, we'd have been in custody."

"How can you be so calm?" he asked, "You just killed someone, then we were shot at. How are you not freaking out?"

"I am freaking out," I replied, with a chuckle, "but letting that control my actions makes a crazy, scary situation worse."

"Where are we going?" he asked as we merged onto the freeway going east.

"We are heading to a little pie shop on highway 26," I said, "I want to make sure we don't have a tail."

"and if we do?" he asked.

"I still have 8 bullets in my gun," I said, "but this is Eastern Washington, you can buy ammo at gas stations."

Jacob just shook his head at my joke.

Chapter 5: Finding Claire

After the sun had set, we returned to town and took the turnoff of the interstate for the lookout. The trip to the pie shop showed that we had no tail or the best tail I'd ever seen. It was about 40 miles from Ellensburg in a small farming community on a lesser-used highway off the interstate.

Given the lack of traffic on the highway, a tail becomes more noticeable. All you have to do is watch the cars that keep with you the whole way and which ones kept following you when you returned. One car followed us all the way, stopping at the gas station across the road from the pie shop but they continued on, showing that we had no tail.

Plus, we got to eat some fantastic pie. Even Jacob enjoyed a slice once he calmed down. I forgot that he did not see what I had done in Rome, I found him Giovanni and the Italian police in the tunnels after I and the girls escaped. Today, I shot the man in front of him.

After Rome, after I killed the men that held me and the girls, I'd had nightmares for weeks, visions of their bodies and visions of what would have happened had I not done what I did, plagued me. Jacob would need time to get over it. As we neared the lookout, I hoped that I could give him that time.

The parking lot of the lookout was empty except for a single pickup truck. I parked our rental a few spots down from it and watched, waiting to see if Mike left the truck. After a moment, the driver's side door to the truck opened and it was Mike, dressed in jeans and a flannel shirt with a cowboy hat.

"That's him," I said to Jacob, patting his leg, "hopefully he has good news."

"You guys sure kicked up a hornet's nest, Sarah," said Mike when I got out of the car, he looked to Jacob, "you could have told me you killed a man at her mom's house."

"Jacob didn't shoot anyone and it was in self-defense," I replied, wondering if I should be offended that he assumed my man did the shooting, "and things would have gotten much worse if you took us in. How's my mom?"

"The Feds from the Seattle Field Office took your mom and stepdad into protective custody," he said, "at least until they figure out what exactly happened. Your mom wouldn't say a word about what happened."

"I shouldn't have come back," I said, my guilt growing, "I shouldn't have believed the letter Claire left me."

"We are looking for her now," said Mike, "she escaped their motel room."

"What?" I asked.

"We caught the man who fled the scene, a neighbor wrote down his license plate number," said Mike, "he had a motel key and we searched the room before the Feds got to town. They had been staying there long term and we found some women's clothes along with an arsenal."

"The motel is across the street from a bank and they gave us the footage from their ATM," he continued, pulling out his phone, "we found her on the footage, she ran off from the motel."

I stared at the picture of the footage displayed on his phone. From the distant black and white footage, I could see that it was a woman with long hair, but I couldn't see her face. There was a possibility it wasn't Claire, but I didn't want to risk that. I couldn't have anyone else hurt because of me.

"What direction did she leave in?" I asked, passing the phone back to Mike.

"East, towards the school," he replied.

"I might know where she is going," I said, "we had a place on campus that we liked to hang out, back in the day. Did the other shooter give you any information?"

"Not to us," he responded, shaking his head, "he had quite the sheet as well and the feds took him in."

"Are they looking for us?" Jacob asked, talking for the first time, "if so, I could make some calls, I still have some favors I can cash."

"Oh, they want some answers," said Mike, "and so do we. There hasn't been a murder in Ellensburg in 20 years. Your little gunfight is bringing national media attention. That said, the feds didn't want your name on anything, Sarah. They aren't sharing anything with us, but I think they have a lot more info on the group that was after you."

"Thank you for all your help," I said, "we are going to try and find Claire, make sure she is ok and then get out of town. Hopefully, with the media attention, the remnants of the Syndicate won't come back looking for me here."

"You gonna tell me why they were after you?" Mike asked, "you were never a girl scout but I'd sure like to know why you have stone cold killers after you."

"I got caught up with the wrong people, the people those men worked for," I said, looking at my hands, "they forced me to work for their organization until I met Jacob who had a plan to destroy them, take their power. The remnants of the organization have been hunting us since."

"I'd feel a lot better if you came in and let us and the feds protect you," he said, "but you seem to be able to handle yourself. Good luck. Come back to visit when it is safe."

"Tell my mom I'm sorry, for everything." I said, "when you see her again."

"I will," he said, nodding before turning and walking back to his car.

I watched him drive away before I turned to Jacob. He pulled me into a hug, squeezing me tightly and patting my back. We stood together like this for a long moment before I pulled away.

"Once I know Claire is safe," I said, "we can get out of here."

"She left the letter," he said, "are you sure she wasn't helping them of her own free will?"

"No, I'm not," I admitted, "but if they did take her, they did it to get to me. I have to find out and make sure she is safe."

The footage Mike showed me, worried me for this reason. After the attack at my mother's house, she conveniently escapes their hotel room. That seemed suspect to me though, given my history with Claire, I wanted to give her the benefit of the doubt.

"And if she is with them?" he asked, "I'm not an idiot, you know. You have more than a professional history with the woman."

"And that was in the past," I replied, shaking my head, "I'm with you now and only you."

"That isn't what worries me," he said, "I'm worried about your objectivity. If you have a blind spot for this woman, you could underestimate her."

"If I find out she helped them willingly, helped them go after my mother," I said, "I'm going to take her down."

"We are going to take her down," he said with conviction in his voice.

I nodded and got into our rental car. Once Jacob joined me, we took off, heading for the university. Like a lot of university campuses, Central Washington University had a network of tunnels underneath it that carried steam, wires and other infrastructure between all of the buildings.

The tunnels were closed off to the public but Claire had a deft hand with lock picking tools and we spent many nights exploring the tunnels. Most of the tunnels contained little of interest but in our exploration, we found a large room, hidden behind a set of shelves.

It had a dusty couch and table inside, empty pull tab beer cans littered the table along with a copy of the first issue of Playboy which had a 1953 date. We guessed that a maintenance man used the room as his secret getaway where he could drink and waste time while at work.

Claire and I cleaned the room up and stole some chairs from a dorm lounge we accessed through the tunnels. It became our secret base of operations. If we needed to hide something, we would store it down there. The tunnels were so rarely used that as long as we avoided them during working hours, nobody would see us coming and going. If Claire wanted to hide from somebody, she would head there.

I parked in the lot next to the library and chuckled as I exited the car.

"What's so funny?" asked Jacob, his eyes weary.

"We don't have a parking pass," I said, "I worried for a moment about getting a parking ticket."

"Yeah, we have bigger things to worry about," he said, "where to?"

"The Art Building has the easiest entrance," I said, pointing towards one of the red brick buildings, "plus it should be open at this hour and the art student building monitors were laxer than those in other buildings, at least they were 8 years ago."

We walked into the Art Building as if we belonged there and after getting my bearings, I made a beeline to the basement door. Finding it locked, I pulled my lock picking tools from my purse and kneeled in front of the door.

"Let me know if you hear anyone coming," I said, sticking the torsion wrench in the lock, "this shouldn't take too long, but I'm a bit out of practice."

I'd set four of the five pins when Jacob shook my shoulder. Footsteps sounded on the stairway above the basement door. I yanked my tools from the lock and pulled Jacob further under the stairwell, where it was darker. A girl carrying a backpack over one shoulder walked down the stairs and continued away from us, through the hall.

Hearing nothing more, I returned to the lock and started over. I unlocked it quickly with no other interruption and stashed my tools once we were on the other side of the closed door. The basement of the art building contained all of the utilities for the building as well as a small supply cache for the janitors with soap, paper towels and toilet paper for the bathrooms of the building.

Before entering the tunnels, I grabbed a large flashlight from the janitorial supplies and passed it to Jacob. His eyes moved from the flashlight to the well-lit tunnel in front of us and he opened his mouth to ask why but I answered before he could.

"Not all the tunnels are as well lit," I said, taking his hand and pulling him towards the tunnel, "and we don't want to be caught in them if the lights go out."

He nodded his acceptance and we started off. Despite not having used the tunnels for years, I quickly remembered where I was heading. Nearing the secret entrance, I slowed to a stop and closed my eyes, trying to hear any sound. Not a peep could be heard.

I approached the set of shelves slowly, each step silent. Jacob emulated as he followed behind me. Again, I heard nothing from the room. I couldn't move the shelves silently but before I pushed them to the side, I pulled the gun from my purse.

"Just in case," I whispered to Jacob when his wide eyes moved to the gun in my hand.

With a shove, I pushed the shelves away from the entrance and peered into the dark room behind them. I heard shuffling from within and Jacob flicked the flashlight on, aiming for the noise.

Claire huddled behind one of the chairs, her dirty blond hair in a mess of curls on her head. She squinted against the beam of the flashlight and sucked in a breath upon seeing me.

"Sarah?" she said, excitement and fear in her voice, "I knew you would come for me."

"You're safe now, Claire," I said, "the men who had you have been arrested."

She stood, confusion blooming on her face. I held the gun in my hand where she couldn't see it. Jacob's words about my possible lack of objectivity fresh in my mind. I didn't want to take any chances.

"Who's he?" asked Claire, venom in her voice.

"This is Jacob," I replied, taking a step forward, still concealing the gun, "we're together."

"He's the one they wanted," she hissed, "they promised me they didn't want to hurt you, that you could go free, go with me."

"And you left that letter in my storage unit to get me to my Mother's house," I said, anger bubbling inside me, "they shot up her house, Claire. She could have died, I could have died."

"I didn't know they were going to do that!" she yelled, "but you can still come with me, we could be together again."

"You think I'm just going to, what, live happily ever after with you," I said, scoffing, "after you almost got my mother killed, almost got Me and Jacob killed?"

"Like you care for him," she said, pointing at Jacob, "men are just marks, remember? You taught me that."

"Things change, Claire," I said, shaking my head, "I love him."

"Love him!" she shrieked, and suddenly she had a pistol in her hands, pointing it towards Jacob.

I stepped in front of him and stared at Claire my own pistol raised. Her eyes widened and her hand began to shake. I prayed that she didn't brush the trigger.

"Claire put the gun down," I said, "don't make me do this."

"You won't shoot me," she said, "you love me."

I didn't have much love for her at the moment, but she was right. I wouldn't shoot her, not if I could help it. This situation required a different tactic.

"Fine, you win," I said, pointing the gun at the ceiling, "I'll go with you, just let Jacob go."

Her eyes widened and a smile burst on her face. She lowered her gun and rushed towards me, opening her arms to hug me. Just before she reached me, I slammed the butt of my pistol into the top of her head with all the anger I'd built up.

She crumpled to the ground with a yowl, holding her head where I hit her with one hand, the other, still clasping the pistol, moved up. I stomped on her wrist until she dropped the gun. Jacob rushed forward and grabbed it, pointing it at Claire.

"Skye might have a soft spot in her heart for you, even after all you did," he growled, "but I do not. Move and I shoot you."

"Roll over onto your stomach, Claire," I said, removing my foot from her wrist.

She stared at me with her hurt eyes but complied, rolling onto her stomach. I fished a pair of handcuffs, covered in pink fur from my purse and clicked them on her wrists.

"Do I want to know why you have fluffy pink handcuffs?" Jacob asked, his gun still pointed at the now sobbing Claire, "You've never brought those out in the bedroom."

"Remember our first time?" I asked back, "I'm not really into bondage but if cops wanted to search my purse a regular pair of handcuffs looks suspicious, these make me look kinky but they are just as good as normal handcuffs."

We led Claire out of the tunnels, emerging from an exterior entrance. While Jacob covered her, I unlatched one of her wrists and handcuffed her to a bench. As we walked back to the car, I texted Mike, telling him where the cops could pick her up. I might not have been able to shoot her, but I wasn't about to let her get away after she helped the remnant of the Syndicate go after my mother.

I started the car and drove straight to the freeway. We'd already overstayed our welcome.

Let's Stay Connected

Hey... this is Aurelia Hilton! Did you enjoy this book? I hope it was steamy & hot and you've absolutely enjoyed this short novel.

You know what? Let's stay connected! I will usually give out copies of my free short novels when I first release them to you, my lovely readers.

It is super simple to stay connected & updated with my future book releases...

Step 1: Join my email list:
http://bit.ly/aureliahiltonjoin

Step 2: Check out my other books! Simply google "Aurelia Hilton erotica books".

Once again, thanks for reading this short novel of mine & let's stay connected! **winks**

CPSIA information can be obtained
at www.ICGtesting.com
Printed in the USA
BVHW031054280819
557040BV00007B/90/P